JACK RANN,

OR

SIXTEEN-STRING JACK,

THE NOBLE-HEARTED HIGHWAYMAN.

THE BARGAIN ON HAMPSTEAD HEATH.

CHAPTER I.

THE MEETING ON THE HEATH.

THE night was dark and dismal, heavy clouds shrouded the heavens, and fitful gusts of wind swept on, with a spitefulness indicative of the coming storm.

It was towards the end of autumn, and the scene of our opening chapter was the famous Hampstead-heath—the resort of many evil-disposed persons and the dread of every traveller journeying to or from the metropolis.

It was night, and, save the sound of the rising wind, nothing was heard in the neighbourhood of the heath.

The hour of midnight had chimed as a well-mouted horseman dashed on the heath from the London-road.

No. 1.

He rode some little distance, and then drew his steed away from the beaten track and listened attentively.

This horseman was a well-formed, well-dressed young fellow, who had perhaps seen some five-and-twenty summers; certainly no more.

His air was extremely jaunty, and a rather pleasant smile played over his features.

The most singular thing about him, however, was, that attached to each boot he wore *eight coloured strings*.

Had you seen him thus decorated and mentioned the fact in any part of Surrey or Middlesex, every nine in ten would have told you that you had encountered no other than SIXTEEN-STRING JACK, the most daring highwayman of the period, so great was his notoriety.

John Rann, or Sixteen-String Jack, was at the period of our tale one of the characters of the day. He was not alone notorious for his wondrous exploits on the road, but for the romantic and chivalrous traits in his character. Bad as he was, and bad as all must have been who followed his profession, there were many redeeming qualities about him which made him a special favourite with numbers of persons, and by the poor, to whom he was very charitable, he was quite idolised.

His life had been from his birth a most singular one, but it is not our intention to go into its details now, as we must confine ourselves for the present to the tale we have undertaken to write, and in which Rann will play a most prominent part.

The horseman, as we before stated, turned his black steed from the road, and drawing her to a standstill, listened attentively. as if in anticipation of the approach of some one.

He waited long and anxiously; becoming at last extremely restless and disturbed.

" Not yet, not yet ! " he cried. " And if he does not come she will die in Newgate. Heaven and earth ! If he should fail me ! Mother hung, child starving—it is too horrible to think of ! "

Muttering such sentences as these, he passed away another half-hour, and then, uttering an exclamation of horror, he continued,—

" If he should have come and gone ! He would seize on the meanest excuse. If I missed him by a minute, he would fly, and I could have no hold on him. But no. The half-hour after midnight was the time appointed, and I know full well that I was before my time. Jack Rann never yet broke his word, or came a moment late in his life; did he pet, did he ? "

This last sentence was addressed to his steed, and the splendid animal evidently knew full well that some kind appeal had been made to it; for, as Jack stooped forward and patted her shoulder, she turned her head and rubbed his hand in the most affectionate manner.

" No, mare ; Jack never broke his word, and it is not likely he would begin at the moment when he is called upon to save the life of a fellow-creature and keep her child from starvation. Bah ! he will come. The bait with which I have tempted him must bring him here ; and, once here, as Heaven is my judge, he shall not leave the spot alive, unless he makes a written confession of his guilt and her innocence. They may tell me that I should not interfere with the concerns of other people ; they may say it will serve me right if I get into trouble over this ; but I care not for their idle word. Let them say, but let me *do* ! I never yet forgot a kindness, and it is too late in life to break off old habits. No, Jack ; do not think of hardening your heart now ; let it rather become still more impressionable, for you do more than sufficient wrong to be easily balanced by a little good on an occasion."

The mare pricked up her ears, and twitched her near fore-leg nervously.

" What is it, old girl ? " asked Jack.

The beautiful mare repeated her movement.

" Again ? What can she mean ? Let me listen ! "

Jack lowered his head and listened in the most attentive manner.

" I hear nothing but the wind. A false alarm this time, old girl. Never mind ; you are so often right that you can afford to be wrong once upon a time."

Again the mare moved about uneasily, and threw back her ears.

" Hilloa, pet ! you do seem obstinate to-night. What is the matter with you ? "

Once more the mare repeated her movement, but this time in a far more decided manner than she had previously done.

" Let me listen again. She may be right after all."

There was a sudden lull of the angry wind, and Rann sought to catch the sounds he expected.

This time he was more fortunate.

Distinctly on his ear fell the sounds of a horse's hoof, beating on the hard road.

" Hurrah ! " shouted Jack. " h comes at last. Now for it."

In another minute a horseman rode rapidly up to the spot opposite which Rann sat on his mare.

Rann just touched his steed with his heel, and she sprang into the road, beside the other horse.

" Hilloa ! " shouted Rann.

" Back," cried the horseman, " back ! I am armed; and if you advance, it will be at the peril of your life."

" Psha ! " cried Rann, " is that the way you treat gentlemen with whom you have appointments ? "

" Who are you ? "

" Jack Rann; or more familiarly speaking, Sixteen-String Jack, entirely at your service."

" You are he who wrote me to meet you here to receive certain documents you were to surrender up ? "

" I am he."

" Then our business is soon over ; let me have them and depart."

" Stop, stop ; we cannot separate thus. Our business over ! Forsooth, it has not yet begun."

" I have no time to waste."

" Mine is also precious ; but you will have to listen to me."

" Not against my inclination."

" Yes, against your inclination."

" What ! Ernest Malvers stay at the bidding of a cut-purse villain—a hunted felon ? "

" Just so. You will have to do precisely what you say. And as to Ernest Malvers ruffling up his feathers at the bidding of Sixteen-String Jack, I can tell him he has stood to many a worse man. Besides, are we not equals ? "

" Equals ! how so ? "

" How so ? Did you not call me a hunted felon ? "

" I did."

" Well ; and perhaps you will have the goodness to inform me what you are ? "

" A gentleman."

" Bah, Ernest Malvers, you too are a felon, although not a hunted one; and you know it. We stand here on equal terms. Now, what have you to say ? "

" I say no man trifles with me."

" And I say the man is not born who ever trifled with me. You put your hand in your pocket ! Mark me, if you draw it out, you are a dead man."

Jack drew a pistol and pointed it at the head of his adversary.

So quick was this done, that it took Malvers by surprise, and he involuntarily drew back a step or two.

" You have weapons in that pocket," said Rann, still keeping his pistol pointed. " Pull out your hand, but do not produce a weapon with it, or, by Heaven, sooner than you can raise your arm a couple of bullets will be crashing through your skull."

Malvers, rather chapfallen, did as he was ordered.

" And now," continued Rann, lowering his pistol, " we can resume our conversation. Where were we ? Oh, I know; we were having some slight dispute about our relative positions; but we will dismiss the theme, and turn to another more interesting to both."

" Ay," said Malvers, " let us be quick, for this is painful to me."

" I am myself on thorns," said Jack ; " but still there is much to be said and done, and we must go through with it steadily, step by step; and painful as it may be to either or both parties, we must miss nothing."

" I do not understand you."

" No, but you will presently."

" I only know that you profess to hold certain papers which are useful to me, and which you have promised to deliver up on receiving the sum of money you have demanded. If you mean to do this, do it at once, and take your reward, for I dare not stay here longer. And, moreover, beyond this, I cannot see what you have to do with me or I with you."

" Oh, all in good time, friend. Never hurry. Now, are you prepared to listen to me ? "

" I have no alternative."

" True, you have not. Now, attention. Five years ago

you were travelling from Canterbury to London by post-chaise. On alighting you dropped some papers, which fell into the possession of the postilion."

"How know you that?"

"Oh, easily enough: I happened to be the postilion. You see I am still on the road, but no longer in the old line. But to resume. The papers you lost were of so much consequence to your liberty and good name that you dared not make inquiry about them, preferring to lose them rather than let the world knew that you were a forger of wills and deeds of transfer. Oh! oh! you start, do you? Poor fellow! I have touched you so nearly, have I?"

"Go on."

"I will. It's rather interesting, is it not?"

"Go on," cried Malvers, impatiently.

"Well, sir, at first I thought I would burn the documents I became possessed of, but I changed my mind. Twelve months afterwards I heard of a death and of an extraordinary will case, in which your name was mixed up. I bethought me of my papers, and said to myself as I glanced over them, ' My friend Malvers has committed a forgery of a will, and the real one, stolen by him and then dropped in the post-chaise, is in my possession. I should be an important witness in the matter, but I shall not bother about it. Let them get over it as they best may. They are all rich, and there will not be much harm done in one member of the family having more than the others.' So, Mr. Malvers, I put my papers back into their resting-place, and allowed things to go on as they chanced, without my assistance."

"Well, well?"

"Well, sir, a few weeks ago the name of Malvers became again familiar to me through reading a singular charge of murder against a lady of that name."

"My wife!"

"Just so—it turned out to be your wife. But do not interrupt. The case was in everybody's mouth, and I could not help being struck by its peculiarity. A poor, harmless, inoffensive woman was accused of committing a most desperate and revolting crime. The evidence against her was circumstantial. Loud groans were heard issuing at midnight from a house in the neighbourhood of Fleet-street. The watch rushed in and found your wife stooping over the mangled body of a youth, who, being identified, proved to be her cousin. This youth, it is said, stood in the way of her becoming possessed of a considerable property, and to remove the obstacle she committed one of the most desperate crimes on record. On being found in the position I described, she was questioned by the officers, and gave so confused an account of the affair, that the suspicions against her rose to certainty. A jury found her 'Guilty,' and a judge sentenced her to death."

"It is so. I believe Augustus Darfield was the object of my wife's bitterest hatred, and I must concur in the justice of the sentence passed on her."

"Villain!" cried Rann, " oh, miserable villain! My soul revolts at holding converse with you; but I will strive to control my passion and finish my task in comparative coolness. Hark ye! In disguise I sought out your wife in the condemned hole of Newgate. I found her there, with her poor innocent babe slumbering in her lap. I saw her anguish, and at a glance I discovered her innocence. I made myself known to her, for she well remembered my parents, heaven rest them! I told her I was prepared to devote myself to her rescue, and drew from her the real facts of the case, which, in pity for you, she had long concealed. She told me that you had drawn Darfield to your house, that you had planned his murder, and that the crime was committed by Francis Austin, another cousin of the murdered man, and, after your wife, the next heir to the property which had long tempted him to crime. She further told me that she knew you were in league with this wretch to effect a division of the property after her death, which you sought to bring about by systematic ill-usage and diabolical cruelties; but that, in spite of all, she had determined to die, and thus save you and your brother murderer from the scaffold. I swore to her that she should be saved, but she made me promise not to compromise you. I am pre-

pared to treat with you now. Write a confession of the murder, regardless of the safety of your wife's cousin, and I will deliver to you the papers by which I tempted you here. Refuse, and I will make you a prisoner, and drag you to justice at the risk of my own neck."

"I will refuse."

"Tempt me not—I am a desperate man!"

"You are a villain, who would endeavour to frighten me into a confession of a crime which was committed by my wife."

"You lie, and you know I speak the truth!"

"I do not know it."

"Tempt me not, I say, or the scaffold shall be your doom."

"Die, dog!" said Ernest Malvers, drawing a pistol from his pocket, and presenting it at Rann's head; but fortunately the flint missed, and no harm done.

In a second Rann was at the throat of his opponent, and grasping him as in a vice of iron, he wrested his weapons from him and left him powerless.

"Fool that you are," cried Jack, " do you think to best me? You are as completely in my power as if every muscle in your body were unstrung. I am your master, and you must obey. I give you five minutes to decide. Will you write the confession, or will you go to Newgate? Mark me, I know where the murderer is to be found, and I will drag him after you. I have a clue which will complete the chain of evidence against you, and nothing can save you. I give you the chance of life at the request of your poor wife. If you do not accept it on the terms I propose you know what will follow."

"Listen, Rann. This woman can be nothing to you. Let me go hence, and keep your tongue quiet, and ten thousand pounds"——

"Cease!" cried Jack; " ten thousand empires would not tempt me. You are mistaking your man. Be certain, I have no inclination to play the villain. Your wife shall be saved— it is for you to say on what terms. You know my determination, so do not play with me beyond my powers of endurance. You have just two minutes more."

"Will nothing tempt you?"

"Have you decided?"

"Rann, spare me!"

"Yes—on the terms proposed."

"Rann, Rann, I will enrich you—I will place you in luxury for the rest of your life—only spare me!"

Rann drew forth a stout cord.

"You have one more minute," he said.

"Oh, Heaven! will nothing tempt you!"

"I am inexorable. Now, the time is up. How is it to be?"

"Must I confess?"

"You must; and you must also give a clue to the whereabouts of your accomplice, and some facts which will lead to an immediate acquittal of your wife."

"I cannot."

The rope was thrown about his body and tightened.

"Oh, Rann—Jack, Jack! Spare me."

"You have had my answer."

"Must I then die a felon's death?"

"You have an alternative."

"I *will write.*"

"Very good; I thought you would."

Jack slackened the rope."

"But there are no writing materials. How can this be done?"

"Oh, I am not unprepared. Here are my tablets. Write."

The man saw that he was completely beaten, and accepting the tablets from Jack, he wrote, with a faltering hand, the following lines:—

"I, Ernest Malvers, do confess that my wife is innocent of the crime for which she is condemned to death. The real culprit, acting on my instigation, is Francis Austin, my wife's cousin, who will be found hiding at 'The Red Rose' beerhouse, in the Minories. We tempted him to my house, and there Austin beat him to death. The clubs he used will be found under some rubbish in the cellarage; together with a part of Austin's coat, which was torn off by the murdered man. The motive which led to this crime was the possession of the property of the murdered man, to which Austin was, after my wife, next heir."

Rann carefully perused this document, and then said,—

"It will do, and here is the will I promised you. It was by that I drew you hither, and I give it you; although I do not know what use it will be to you, as you will have to quit England immediately. However, that is not my business. I made a promise, and I always keep my word. Adieu."

Rann handed Malvers a bundle of papers, and setting his horse in motion galloped away over the heath, leaving the brutal husband gazing after him in extreme bewilderment.

CHAPTER II.

THE CONDEMNED HOLE OF NEWGATE.

IN the famous condemned hole of Newgate Gaol, on the night of the opening of our tale, sat a young and, despite the awfully careworn features, very beautiful female. On her knee lay an infant, on which she gazed with extreme tenderness. It was her own darling boy.

"God bless and protect you, my poor, innocent babe," she said; "In a few hours you will be motherless, and cast on the mercy of a cold and friendless world. I commend you to your Heavenly Father's care, for he who gave you birth has cruelly deserted both you and your poor broken-hearted mother."

The poor creature burst into a flood of passionate tears, and drawing her child close to her, moaned and wept over him for more than an hour.

She was interrupted by the entrance of the chaplain of the prison, a fine, elderly gentleman, whose face bespoke the goodness and greatness of his heart.

He approached her gently, and laying his hand affectionately on her head, spoke to her in a calm and sweet voice, which at once arrested her tears and somewhat composed her perturbed feelings.

"Daughter," he said, "the hours pass quickly; it is after midnight, and the fatal hour approaches with a swiftness which will soon place thee over the gap which lies between thee and another world. It is time that we turn our thoughts heavenward, and cease to grieve over the affairs of this world. It is ordained that thou shalt suffer; it is meet that thou dost bow to His will without a murmur, for He in His infinite wisdom knoweth what is good for thee."

"'Tis well, sir," she murmured, "but I do not weep for myself; it is for my poor babe. Oh, I cannot leave him thus without a murmur! It is not in human nature for a mother to quite her child, her first and only one, without a murmur. It may be good for him, it may be good for me, Mr. Ashton; but, oh, it is hard, very hard, to teach the heart that lesson."

"It is, my poor child, it is; but thou shouldst try."

"I do try, sir, indeed I do; but it is all without avail. May I ask, sir, has any one inquired after me?"

"No, daughter; didst thou expect any one?"

"Yes, sir; I did expect—a friend."

"To take leave of you?"

The poor woman was silent.

"I see," continued the chaplain, "you yet hope for a reprieve. Oh! dismiss the thought. It is idle to hope; believe me, there is no earthly chance. I have done my best for thee. I have petitioned the minister. I have sent a most influential deputation to him, but he will not move in the matter. The answer is, that the law must take its course."

"Ah, they do not believe me innocent?"

"No, child, they do not."

"But you, Mr. Ashton, you cannot think me guilty?"

"It is impossible to be long with thee and entertain the faintest suspicion. No, my daughter, I would stake my life on your innocence; but it is very hard to make the world believe as I think."

"And I shall die?"

"God has willed it so."

"Then Heaven have mercy on me!"

"Amen."

The poor creature, who, as the reader will easily imagine, was no other than Malver's ill-fated wife, bowed her head over her child, and gazing on it tenderly, again burst forth into a flood of tears.

"Who, who will give thee a crust of bread, though thou should starve, after I am gone?" she cried. "Oh, my poor, darling babe, who will succour thee?"

"I will," said the chaplain; "yes, my poor soul, I will. I have no child of my own, and I will adopt thy little one, and love it as if it were born to me. I am not rich, but I have enough for him and me."

"Oh, Heaven bless you for those words, sir; they are balm to my bruised heart. Heaven bless and reward you for your goodness."

"It will, it has. Charity brings with it its own reward; the pleasure of doing good is sufficient satisfaction to the Christian."

"Now," cried Mrs. Malvers, "now I feel that I can pray with you, sir; my heart is more at ease."

The poor soul placed her child on the hard couch, and fell on her knees beside it.

"Father," she said, "I am resigned to thy will: let it be done."

There was a noise behind her which attracted her attention. Turning, she beheld an old man with long white hair and beard; he was habited in a loose surtout which reached his ankles, and completely disguised his figure.

The gaoler accompanied him, and said to Mrs. Malvers—

"Here is an old man who says he knows you. He can remain with you half an hour. I will not wait. The presence of the chaplain will be sufficient."

The man withdrew, and turning the key in the lock, went away.

Mrs. Malvers gazed at the new comer for an instant, and then exclaimed——

"I do not know you, sir."

"Hush," said the old man, coming close to her, and whispering in her ear; "it is I, Jack Rann."

Mrs. Malvers started.

Collecting herself, she said,—

"You can speak; Mr. Ashton will not betray you."

"Who are you, sir?" cried Mr. Ashton, unable to understand this strange scene.

"Oh, sir," said Mrs. Malvers, "he is an old acquaintance, who seeks to save me. He is unfortunate, and is hunted by the authorities. He dares not reveal himself for fear of detection; you will not betray him."

"Heaven forbid, if he is in thy service," said Mr. Ashton.

"I would and will save her," said Rann. "Hark ye, sir, here are the proofs of her innocence. It is the confession of one of the real culprits, who has escaped from the power of the law. The other, as you will see, may be traced by the instructions therein given. Will you exert yourself for her?"

"I will," cried Mr. Ashton, rapidly glancing over the paper, "I will. Yes, yes; if there be but time to get to the office of the Secretary of State for the Home Department and see him. The work of death can be stopped, and the guilty brought to justice."

"My husband!" cried Mrs. Malvers. "Jack, Jack, you have betrayed him and deceived me!"

"Do not accuse me wrongfully," cried Rann "I have saved you, but he is free."

"He has escaped?"

"Yes; by this time he is far away. I do not think they will trace him."

"Heaven bless you for that!"

"Oh, don't thank me, Mrs. Malvers; I swore to save you at all risks. Your husband complied with requests which placed him beyond danger. Had he refused to obey me, I would, even at the risk of incurring your bitter hatred, have dragged him to the scaffold, and forced him, on the fatal drop, to rescue you from a death you did not deserve."

"You are a good and brave man," said the chaplain, tapping Rann approvingly on the shoulder, "and I admire you."

And then, remembering that he was addressing a criminal, and evidently a notorious one, he continued, "At least you are brave, if you are not good."

"Oh, sir," said Rann, "I am well enough, as men go. I might be better, and I might be worse; at all events, I am not the man to see the innocent suffer for the guilty."

"But," said Mr. Ashton, "this is a waste of time; we must away. How shall I get to the minister's house?"

"How!" cried Jack, "why, jump up behind me on my mare, and I will fly with you."

"It is a matter of life and death."

"It is; and I will whisper it to the mare, and you shall see how well she understands the importance of the mission."

"Adieu, my child," cried the chaplain. "If we do not return in time, commend thy soul to heaven."

"If we do not return in time! By Jove, chaplain, you don't know what sort of stuff my mare is made of."

CHAPTER III.

MALVERS PUTS THE MURDERER ON THE SCENT—JACK ON THE WATCH—A LIFE AND DEATH STRUGGLE.

MALVERS remained in the position we described at the end of the first chapter for some moments. His senses had almost deserted him, but making a gigantic struggle to rid himself of the oppression under which he laboured, he at length shook it off.

"It is like a dream," he cried; "it is like a hideous, incomprehensible dream. Would that I had been dreaming!"

He glanced on the papers he still held in his hand.

"Alas!" he continued, "alas for the sad reality! Who is this fiend, this Jack Rann, who has started up in my path and marred my plans? Oh, he shall suffer for this before I have done with him! But now I must take action. Another hour, and my confession will be in the hands of the authorities. My wife will live, Austin will die in her stead, and if I do not fly I shall share his doom. What can be done? Ah! a sudden thought. If I could but rescue Austin the authorities will imagine the paper to be a vile forgery, planned for the purpose of rescuing the condemned woman, and they will not revoke the sentence. It is a desperate hazard; but if successful, all would be well. The stake is worth playing for, and I will make the attempt. Yes, yes; to the Minories — to the Minories!"

The horseman goaded on his horse in the direction Rann had taken.

The beast, frantic with pain, appeared to fly over the heath like a winged creature.

The stones flew from under its hoofs, and still the lash was applied and the spurs used.

"On, on!" shouted Malvers, "hey, on! It is life or death! On, on!"

He shouted and screamed like a madman, and urged his steed along at a truly terrible pace. One false step, one stumble, would have ended his career; but he thought of nothing but the task in hand.

He saw only a halter before his eyes, and he determined to evade it at all risks.

Thus he argued with himself:—

"Rann will seek out some one to execute his commission for him. They will have to go to Newgate, thence to the authorities, thence for the officers, and thence slowly to the Minories. If I can but make this beast sustain its pace I shall be there a full hour before them—I can snatch Austin from their grasp, and my wife will pace the scaffold in a few hours."

Again he applied the whip, again he yelled to his horse, and urged it on at the top of its speed.

The poor creature became bathed in foam, but it was a remorseless horseman on its back. It was a crime-stained man driven to desperation who urged it forward.

The thought of an ignominious end was in his mind's eye, and he hesitated not to evade it at all risks and under all cir-

cumstances. He killed men, and could not, therefore, be expected to care for the death of a poor horse. The blood spurting from its side was naught to him. He had seen the crimson tide flow from wounds in the human body, and he shuddered not.

"To the Minories!"

That was his only thought.

How he got there was naught to him.

But there was an avenger on the track. There was a man as desperate and determined as himself working against him; and we have yet to see in whose favour the game of life and death terminated.

*　*　*　*　*　*

Jack's mare flew over the ground, to the utter consternation of the good old chaplain, who, in all probability, was never before placed in a position so novel and perilous.

There he was, on a blood mare, his arms encircling the waist of a daring highwayman, positively flying through the streets of London in the dead of the night, bound on an errand of life and death. They were *en route* for the West-end of London, where the principals of the Home Department of the Government resided.

That there should be no hitch, no delay, the chaplain had concluded to trust to no one but himself; and deeming it advisable to at once place the facts in the possession of the First Minister of the department, he at once rode to his residence, determined that nothing should prevent him from obtaining an audience, late as the hour was.

The minister resided in St. James's-street, and thither Rann hurried his splendid mare. Down Ludgate-hill, up ill-paved and still worse lighted Fleet-street, with its oil-lamps swinging to and fro in the night-wind, and its croaking watchman drawling forth the hour of the night, and assuring the peaceful citizens who chanced to break their slumbers that "all was well;" through the Strand, by Charing-cross, into Pall-mall, filled with chairmen and lacqueys—for it was the height of the London season, and the West-end was in its full glory—and thence to St. James's-street, where were to be seen a still greater collection of chairmen, many blazing flambeaux, and throngs of bedizened servants; for the Minister of the Home Department was that night entertaining a large party of his friends and partizans at dinner, with cards and the inevitable *soirée.*

Through these things Jack had to pick his way as he best could; and for a man presenting his appearance (it must be remembered that he still wore the garb and beard in which he ventured within the precincts of Newgate,) he created a noise which surprised his hearers into admiration of his powerful lungs.

Several watchmen endeavoured to retard his progress, but the sight of the chaplain assured them that all was well, and that the errand of the noisy rider of the blood mare was not to be checked.

After a struggle our hero succeeded in gaining the door of the house he sought.

"Dismount," he said to the chaplain; "there is not a moment to be lost. Waste no more time than is necessary for her life hangs but on the merest thread."

"Trust me," said the chaplain. "I am alive to the vital importance of the errand."

He sprang to the ground, and hurried into the entrance-hall of the house.

Here he was accosted by a bevy of servants, who demanded his business.

"My business is with Lord Lismouth," said the chaplain.

"I fear you cannot see him to-night," said the servant, with respect in his tone, "for his lordship is much engaged."

"Of that I have no doubt," said the chaplain; "but my business is of the most imperative nature. I am chaplain of Newgate, and life and death depend upon my interview with his lordship. Pray tell him this, and you will oblige me."

"I will convey the message," said the servant, "but I fear his lordship will refuse to see you."

"I have no such fears," said the good old priest; and the servant departed on his mission.

During his absence, the chaplain engaged himself by gazing at the stream of light which filled the grand hall in which he stood, and in listening to the melody and laughter which reached him from the upper apartments.

"No wonder," he said, "that these great ones have so little thought for the poor wretches amongst whom my life is passed; for what is there in common between this scene and the one I have just quitted? Nothing, nothing! It is hard to bring the mind to believe that such a mighty contrast could be found within a circle so small."

The servant returned, and beckoning the chaplain to follow him, said—

"His lordship will grant you an interview, sir. Pray follow me."

The man led the way to a small retiring-room in the neighbourhood of the brilliant suite of apartments thrown open to his lordship's guests.

"Remain here, sir, and his lordship will be with you presently," said the man, immediately withdrawing.

In a few minutes the minister, a fine old gentleman with a truly noble cast of countenance and distinguished bearing, entered the room.

Without the slightest preliminary remark he commenced business.

"Now, sir," he said, "I understand you have important business with me. I need not say that this is not the place and time for business, because I am convinced that you are well acquainted with the fact, and that you would not intrude if you had not sufficient excuse for doing so."

"You are right, my lord," said the chaplain; "I should not have intruded on your privacy without sufficient excuse, and I will take care to be as brief as I possibly can, now that you have done me the favour of receiving me. There is in Newgate a poor woman under sentence of death, and whose execution is fixed for to-morrow."

"Ah, you refer to Mrs. Malvers; a very sad case, Mr. Chaplain, a very distressing case; but I trust, after the very decided manner in which I have already expressed my views on that matter, that your business is not to further importune me in her behalf?"

"I am here to ask a reprieve for her, my lord, but not on grounds of former applications."

"Then I may at once tell you, sir, that unless you have convincing proofs of her entire innocence of the crime with which she is charged you do wrong to come here, for my mind is made up on the point."

"I think I have proofs which will satisfy your lordship that I do not come here without sufficient reason. Will your lordship do me the favour of reading this paper?"

The chaplain drew forth the confession and placed it in the minister's hands.

Lord Lismouth gave a rapid glance over the scrawl.

"How was this obtained?" he asked, as he finished the perusal of the document.

The chaplain had no wish to reveal the source by which the confession came into his hands, and so endeavoured to evade the question.

"It was brought to Mrs. Malvers to-night by one who had just left her cruel husband."

"Where is this husband?"

"That we do not know."

"Really, sir, this is most suspicious," said the minister; "the document may be a clever forgery, produced by some friend of the unhappy woman who lies under sentence. I do not think I should regard it in any serious light."

"For the love of God," cried the clergyman, "do nothing hastily. On my veracity I believe that document to be valid. Of the innocence of the poor woman I am well convinced, and if she perishes, my lord, her blood will be upon your head alone."

"You speak warmly."

"Oh, yes; but pardon me, my lord, I feel deeply on the subject, and cannot tutor my tongue to set phrases. Oh, believe me, this unhappy woman is as innocent as your own wife of the crime with which she is charged and for which she is condemned to suffer. That paper reveals all, and to treat it as a fabrication is to wilfully destroy a precious life. If I were not fully convinced of this, I should not be standing in your presence on this occasion."

"You see, sir," said Lord Lismouth, "my responsibility is a great one, and I have no wish to abuse the power I wield. I grant that you believe this woman innocent, but I have no real *facts* before me. There is your *belief* and a pencilled scrawl, which might have been written by the prisoner herself, for aught I know. There is no witness's signature. There is no one to vouch for its authenticity. Under these circumstances it only rests with me to grant a provisional reprieve."

"A provisional reprieve?"

"Yes. If you can produce either the husband or the cousin of this woman before the time of execution, the sentence shall be delayed."

"But if he should have escaped?"

"I can do no more."

"Think, my lord, oh think of the awful responsibility which rests upon you! Think that if, as we reach the scaffold with the real culprit, we see the fatal bolt drawn, and the innocent victim launched into eternity, you alone are to blame. Oh, think of this. Delay the execution for a day, in order that the innocent may have a chance of life."

"It is not in my power to do so," said the minister; "and I still think that you are imposed upon, and that this woman is the real culprit. Take this."

The minister had written something on a paper, which he now handed to the chaplain. It ran as follows:—

"To the Governor of Newgate.

"You are hereby empowered to delay the execution of the woman now lying in Newgate under sentence of death, for the murder of Augustus Darfield; provided that Francis Austin or Ernest Malvers, persons presumed to be implicated in the crime, be placed in your charge before the hour of execution.

(Signed)   "LISMOUTH."

As the chaplain glanced over this order his heart failed him.

"Heaven help her," he cried; "her doom seems sealed."

"There is no help for it," said Lord Lismouth. "It would, you may rest assured, be more pleasing to me to see this poor wretch live than die; but I have a duty to perform for those who have placed the authority of the office I hold in my hands. Society must be protected, and I trust I shall never fail in my duty."

"Amen," said the chaplain; "but, my lord, there may be such a thing as too much zeal. God grant that this case may not prove illustrative of the fact. I humbly take my leave."

The poor old chaplain withdrew.

"Umph!" said the minister, as he prepared to return to his guests, "umph! A stupid old man, that. I wonder who selected him for the office of chaplain of Newgate."

No matter who did so. Certain it was that no better representative of the office could have been found.

His lordship returned to his friends, and soon forgot that there was such a place as Newgate in the world.

The chaplain retraced his steps to the street, and there found Jack awaiting his return.

"You have been an intolerably long time," cried Jack; "but what cheer—what hope?"

"But little, I fear."

The chaplain then recounted the substance of his interview with Lord Lismouth.

"Little hope!" said Jack, as the narrative was brought to an end; "little hope!—bah; you know nothing of the matter. There's every hope."

The chaplain shook his head.

"You think not," said Jack; "but we shall see. I never failed a friend, and the mare never failed me. All you have to do is to hold on, and keep as close to me as possible. Now, then, for the Minories. On, mare! Ahoy,—ahoy, girl!"

The shout was sufficient. The bonny mare bounded forward, and was soon retracing her steps in the direction of the City. Quick as she had flown to the West-end, her pace had been nothing to that at which she now covered the ground.

It appeared to the chaplain that the houses flew past him in one continuous wild flight. All was confused and dim. The lights danced past him, and things lost their natural forms.

In his ears rang the clatter of the mare's hoof's as she dashed fire from the rough flint-stones in her mad gallop, and the excited voice of Rann, encouraging the steed onward.

"Hoy, mare—good mare—on, on—hey up—hey up—on on. Hiss-s-s! up, up—hey! on!"

At every fresh shout the mare tossed up her splendid head, as if in token of recognition of the orders she received.

Her nostrils were extended, and foam broke out all over her sleek body. Her eyes were filled with wild excitement, and despite the heavy burden she bore, there was no diminution of the speed, no relaxation of a muscle. On, on, she sprang, as lightly and gracefully as a fawn.

Onward, to the dark, dangerous, and terrible precincts of the Minories—the quarter of the very worst thieves and cut-throats of London.

Sure-footed as a racer on a well-kept course, she continued her way, extending her limbs to the utmost, and bounding on, nearer and nearer the goal.

The instinct of the animal taught it that extraordinary efforts were expected, and being used to the excitement of the flight and the chase, it seemed to thoroughly appreciate the position in which it was now placed, and strove with might and main to win the approval of its master.

Rann used neither whip nor spur; his shouts were sufficient to urge his mare onward. At the sound of his voice she would redouble her efforts, and at length dashed into Lagsman-street, in which place was situated the "Red Rose" public house, a den for thieves and rascals of the worst class.

"This is the place," said Jack, as he drew rein at the door of as repulsive a house of entertainment as one would wish to enter.

"What do you purpose doing?" asked the chaplain.

"You will see. Dismount."

Jack and Mr. Ashton sprang to the ground at the same moment.

"I will enter," said Jack. "If Dick Turpin or Tom King should chance to be within, they will lend me a hand; if not, I must do the task by myself."

"What task?"

"What task? Why, the seizing of Austin. I'd drag him out though he were in the centre of an army."

"You will not attempt to enter the house without the assistance of officers of justice?"

"Officers of justice! Show me one who would dare enter that house with hostile intentions."

"Is it, then, so dangerous?"

"It is death to anyone who is not branded with the stamp of crime. Hush!"

"What do you hear?"

"I hear nothing."

"But I do. It is the tramp of a horse—an unusual sound in this neighbourhood. Let us draw on one side and see what is in the wind. Silent, mare!"

Jack, the chaplain, and the mare, the latter making but the faintest sounds as she moved over the stones, stole away into the shadow of the houses, at some slight distance from the inn.

In a few moments they beheld a horseman, hot with haste, dash up to the door of the inn, and, dismounting, demand admittance.

"Hilloa!" said Jack, in a whisper, to his companion, "hilloa! there's a nice game a' foot here."

"Who is it?"

"Who is it? Why, Malvers, come to put Austin on the scent."

"Unfortunate."

"Not at all. Quite the reverse."

"What do you mean?"

"Simply that to drag Austin from the house would have been a task of the greatest magnitude, but to seize him as he comes out will be comparatively easy work."

"But are you assured he will come out?"

"From what other purpose but to bring him from danger is Malvers here?"

"True—true."

"Hush! they have admitted him; now for work."

Jack touched his mare, and then stole back to the house, outside which the horse ridden by Malvers stood motionless. Jack applied his whip to the jaded brute, and it galloped off with all the haste it could make.

"So! we win the first move. His horse is gone, and now we shall see if we can't have him."

"Pray do no violence."

"Violence! How shall we deal with violent men if not by violent measures? However, the work is not for you. Stand back, and let me do the task alone."

Jack approached the door of the house and applied his ear to the keyhole.

"Hist!" he said, "they come. Now for it."

He drew his pistols, and stood prepared for what was to follow.

Withdrawing a pace, he watched the opening of the inn door.

Malvers, accompanied by a young man, who proved to be Austin, sprang through the doorway and into the street.

It was the work of a moment, for the proprietor of the "Red Rose" did not allow unwelcome guests the chance of entering his premises without his sanction; but, quick as the movement of opening and shutting the door had been accomplished, the men who had effected egress had not time to move two paces before Jack had confronted them.

"Stand!" cried Rann, presenting his pistols.

"To whom?" shouted Austin, raising a pistol he bore in his hand.

"To Jack Rann, the avenger of Darfield."

"Back, fool," cried Malvers; "back, or we fire upon you."

"Fly, Ernest Malvers," shouted Rann, "I have nought to do with thee. Fly, it is with this villain I have business."

"I will never desert him," cried Malvers.

"Then you must share his fate, for he shall be in Newgate before another hour has passed over his head."

Malvers attempted to beat down Jack's weapons, and at the same moment Austin fired.

The bullet passed through Jack's left arm, but he moved not.

Discharging his pistols at the pair, but without effect, our hero clubbed one of the weapons and rushed at Austin. They struggled until they reached the road, close to the spot where Jack's mare stood.

At this point Malvers skulked behind the highwayman, and dealing him a tremendous blow on the head sent him to the earth, and he fell under the mare.

At this moment Malvers, seeing lights in the street, turned and fled. Austin now grasped his second pistol, and, cocking it, was taking deliberate aim at his prostrate foe, when Jack's mare seized him with her teeth by the shoulder and forced him to drop the weapon.

Austin howled with pain and endeavoured to drag himself from the hold of the mare, but the faithful creature clung to him with the tenacity of a bull-dog.

Meanwhile Jack shook off the effects of the blow he had received and sprang to his feet.

He at once grappled with Austin, and seizing him with his left hand held his throat until he was well nigh suffocated.

Meanwhile the lights kept approaching, and it became apparent that the whole force of the night watch was bearing down to the spot

"Fly," said Jack, to the terrified chaplain, "fly, or it will be too late."

He sprang on the back of his mare as he spoke, and dragged the almost inanimate body of Austin after him.

In a moment the mare dashed away, and the stupefied chaplain was surrounded by a crowd of modern Dogberries.

CHAPTER IV.

FOLLOWS JACK AND HIS PRISONER.

AWAY flew the black mare, and Jack, without bestowing a second thought on the chaplain, dashed in the direction of Newgate.

THE MARE SAVES THE LIFE OF SIXTEEN-STRING JACK.

He had seized his prey, and that was all he cared for.

"Ah!" he cried, "I have you now, and she is saved."

"Whither are you taking me?" cried Austin, as soon as he recovered his reason.

"To the gallows, man, to the gallows."

"Oh, prithee, release me," cried the abject wretch, finding himself powerless, "prithee release me. I never did you harm."

"Maybe not, but you have committed murder, and you would allow one who is good and innocent to mount the gallows in your stead. That one, a poor helpless woman, I honour and love as dearly as though she were my own sister. I have registered an oath to snatch her from the gallows and place thee in her position. I have said, and I will do it."

"Listen, I am rich, I will"—

"Silence, lest I cheat the hangman of his due by strangling thee at once. Silence, and tempt me not, for it is useless."

Rann directed the course of his mare to Newgate, and there, after a gallop of a few minutes, he drew rein.

Without hesitation he sprang from his horse, still holding the murderer in his grasp, and applied himself to the knocker at the principal entrance.

It was now almost daylight, and the authorities of the prison being astir, the pair were admitted, the mare following Jack through the gates.

"What! Mr. Jack Rann voluntarily inside the gates o' Newgate?" said the turnkey, "Vel, this here is rum. Why, what game is up?"

"A bad one. Here, I've turned honest, and taken to your own trade; see what a brute I've brought you as a commencement."

"Why, who is this gentleman?" asked the turnkey.

"Who? Why the murderer of Darfield."

"Vot, the cove as Mrs. Malvers is a going to swing for at eight?"

"The same, only this gentleman's presence saves Mrs. Malvers the trouble of going through the ceremony."

"Vel," said the turnkey, "you alvays vos a rum bird, and there vos never no getting at yer; but you had best come before the deputy-governor."

"All right," said Jack, pushing the now utterly speechless and dejected Austin before him, "but give an eye to the mare."

"Oh, she shall be all right. I say, Jack, it was rather soft of you to come here, after all. You won't require the mare again in a hurry."

"Oh, sha'nt I? We shall see."

"So we shall, Jack."

They now approached the office of the deputy-governor, and entered it without ceremony.

It was a curious place, was that office.

The walls were of coarse plaster, and the only adornments were a variety of instruments usually carried by those who uphold the majesty of the law.

Over the fireplace was an enormous blunderbuss, attached to which was a card, on which was printed the word "LOADED."

THE REPRIEVE.

is a warning to those who approached it to keep their hands off.

Near this instrument of death were a number of pistols of every possible size and shape.

The next conspicuous articles were the swords and hangers, which looked remarkably bright and dangerous as they glistened on the walls.

Then the eye fell on a variety of sticks, staves, and bludgeons; and above all on a score pair of handcuffs, or " darbies," many of which had doubtless graced the wrists of some of the most notorious criminals of the generation.

At a desk in this singular apartment, poring over the last number of the "Hue and Cry," was the deputy-governor of Newgate—a small, bustling little gentleman, dressed in a suit of shabby brown, and shoes all the worse for wear, and face and hands all the more repulsive for absence of soap and water.

Flitting about this important luminary, there were a number of smaller stars in the shape of gaolers, thieftakers, and watchmen, all of whom exhibited a repugnance to the keen morning air by drawing as near the fire as possible.

"Hillo," said the deputy-governor, " and who have we here, so early in the morning?"

"Why, no!" shouted several of the officers in a breath. "It is—it can't be—and yet it is—SIXTEEN-STRING JACK!"

"Yes, it is I," said Rann; "and what do you make of that?"

It was evident that the limbs of the law could make nothing at all of that, and so they contented themselves by staring from one to the other, and ejaculating—

"Why, no, it can't be! How queer!" and other interjections of a similar stupid nature.

"Why, what has brought you here, Jack Rann?" asked the deputy, glaring at Jack from over his spectacles.

"I have brought you a murderer," said Jack. "Behold the destroyer of the man Darfield!"

"Why, Jack, what do you mean? Mrs. Malvers killed Darfield."

"Nothing of the kind; this is the real murderer. Mr. Ashton will explain all."

"Mr. Ashton! what has he to do with it?"

"Everything; he has procured a reprieve for Mrs. Malvers, on condition that this brute be brought here; and here I have brought him."

"But where is the reprieve? where is Mr. Ashton?"

"Where?" echoed Jack. "Oh, good God! he should have been here by this."

"Where did you leave him?"

"In the Minories!"

"And you expect to see him here?"

"Fool that I am! What have I done now?"

"Well, you have not done much unless you can produce the reprieve or Mr. Ashton. We can't stop an execution on your word, Jack."

"True, true; but he will come."

"Are you sure he did not fall into the hands of the gang?" asked the deputy.

"More probably into the hands of the watch, for they were upon him when I fled."

"Just as bad. He will be taken to some remote watch-house, and before anything could be done eight o'clock will have tolled from St. Paul's, and the bolt will have fallen."

"No, no!" cried Jack in an agony of terror, "that must not be. You cannot sacrifice an innocent woman like that. I am sure you will delay the execution until the return of the chaplain."

"We will do nothing of the kind. The under-sheriff will be here at half-past seven, and at eight Mrs. Malvers will die, unless Lord Lismouth's reprieve, if there be such a thing, is in our hands."

"Oh, Heaven!" cried Jack, "what shall I do?"

"Well, I do not see that you can do much, Jack, for you see you are yourself a prisoner."

"No, no!" said Jack; "you would not be so cruel as to deprive the poor woman of one chance of life. You will let me go forth again to complete the work I have begun."

"I don't know about that. There is something strange about the case. How do we know but what Mr. Ashton has been purposely thrust out of the way, and this tale trumped up to gain time for projecting some plot or other? No, no, Jack, we can do little for you."

"But you will let me seek Mr. Ashton?"

"No."

"No! Oh, do not, do not say that."

"Why, Jack, you have forgotten one thing that will save the life of the woman."

"Have I? Have I? Name it."

"It is the confession of your prisoner. If he confesses the crime, there would be an end to the bother."

"True," said Jack, turning to Austin, "true; and now, man, if there is one spark of humanity left in you, confess your crime, and save the poor soul who lies below, suffering in mind and body for your infamous deed. Confess, confess!"

"I have nothing to confess," said Austin. "All I know is, that I was violently attacked by this man in the Minories, and dragged here, I know not wherefore. This is, as you suspect, some infamous attempt to save a guilty woman. I beg you will place this man under restraint and set me free."

"Not so fast," said the deputy; "all in good time, young man. If you are innocent, you will not mind being detained here a few hours."

"But I do mind. My business"—

"Your business cannot be very important, or you would not be found in the Minories at the hour at which you confess to have been there; so say nothing on that score. Look here, Jack. It appears to me that, after all, there is something in your tale. You are too old a bird to thrust yourself inside these gates without sufficient cause, and so I am inclined to give some credence to the assertions that you utter."

"Bless you for that," said Jack; "that is kind of you."

"Now," pursued the deputy, "they say that the chief peculiarity of Jack Rann is, that he never yet broke his word"—

"It is so, or I should not have been here now."

"Good. On the faith of that saying I am inclined to allow you to pass without the prison. Before you go you must swear to me that you will devote yourself only to the business you have in hand, and that as soon after eight o'clock as possible you will deliver yourself up to me, a prisoner, on the many charges I have here booked against you."

"This I cheerfully swear. I would desire nothing better," said Jack.

"Then you can go, and, if your errand be as good a one as I believe it to be, God speed you."

There was, after all, a heart beating under that dirty cuticle; one would not have thought it, on getting a first glimpse at the hard features and cold grey eyes: but there are singular contrarieties in human nature, and a water may, perchance, make a mistake when glancing at some types of the human countenance.

"I shall be back before eight," said Jack, "either bringing with me the proofs of Mrs. Malvers' innocence, or ready to die with her on the scaffold."

"Not so bad as that, Jack," said the deputy; "we shall let you off this time, with something less than a halter."

"I trust so," said Jack.

As he passed into the prison-yard, the clock struck six.

"Two hours!" said Rann, "two hours! Heaven and earth, mare! what have we not to do in that time!"

As soon as Jack was gone, the deputy ordered the gaolers to lock up the suspected man.

"Why am I to be used thus?" asked Austin. "Is the word of a common cut-throat and desperate highwayman to be taken before mine?"

"No matter," said the deputy, "no matter. There will be plenty of time for you to assert your innocence hereafter; and, before you go, a word of advice in your ear. If you would desire to make old officials believe in your innocence, don't conduct yourself as you are now doing—your actions being as unlike those of an innocent man as anything I ever beheld in my long experience."

"Indeed!"

"Yes, indeed!"

"You are a most impertinent old fool," said Austin, "and you will regret this conduct."

"Perhaps so. I have regretted many things in my time; it will be no novelty to me."

"I shall inform the Governor of——"

"Pooh! away with him! we want no such stuff here."

Mr. Austin found himself rather roughly handled, and thrust away into a cell, without further ceremony. Newgate is not, and never was, a place where etiquette was particularly well observed.

* * * * * *

Turn we now once more to that condemned hole wherein the poor woman and her child lay shivering in the cold.

It had struck six, and still no appearance of Rann—still no sign of Mr. Ashton.

"They have failed!" she cried, her poor swollen eyes again overflowing with tears; "they have failed, and dare not come to me. Oh God! what shall I do? In two hours—two short hours, I must leave thee, my poor lamb. I must quit thee, and seek a world where all is good and just; but I leave thee branded as the child of a murderess, to fight with a world which will have no sympathy with thee. God protect thee and watch over thee, for I must die."

Then she pressed her poor babe to her heart, and covered it with kisses. She deprived herself of much of her scant clothing to protect it from the chilly air, but as she did so her tears would break forth again, for the thought of who would do that for her infant when her eyes were closed in death came upon her, and the image of her darling—pale, emaciated, neglected, scorned—presented itself to her mind's eye.

Then came one ray of hope. She had heard of people being snatched from the very scaffold; she had read of persons rescued from the stony grasp of death.

Why should not this be her case?

But the gloom gathered again, and she saw no hope—not one little ray to gladden her.

Meanwhile, the moments stole away, and the fatal hour of eight was fast approaching.

And neither Jack nor Mr. Ashton came to her.

Without the gaol was assembling a vast throng of people to witness the execution.

Such a crowd as can only be seen at such places was gathering there. A wild, godless, fearless, cruel gang, who awaited the coming sight as a treat of the highest order.

As their yells rose and their number increased, so died out hope; and death—death was staring the innocent woman in the face.

CHAPTER V.

THE CHAPLAIN—THE REPRIEVE—THE MIRACULOUS ESCAPE FROM THE LOCK-UP.

"HILLO!" said one of the many watchmen who surrounded the chaplain; "hillo! what's the meaning of all this riot?"

"It's nothing; at least nothing that I can explain. I pray you let me pass. Do not detain me. A life hangs upon me."

"What a pity, to be sure!" said the watchman, with mock sympathy. "Who'd have thought it? Let you go! You must think us green."

"You certainly will not detain me."

"Oh, won't we?—we shall see about that. Bring him along."

"I implore, I entreat you, not to detain me. I have done nothing to warrant detention, and must implore you to release me."

"That's all very fine, my friend, but it will not do for us. You must come away to the lock-up."

"No, no; I cannot remain here another moment. Life and death hang upon my presence elsewhere."

"Dear me, that's very distressing; but, unfortunately, we are too old to be caught with such chaff; so come along."

"Whither will you drag me?"

"To the lock-up in Aldersgate-street."

"For the love of Heaven, do not serve me thus! Do you not see that I am a minister? Is not my cloth sufficient to protect me from such insult and degradation?"

"Not if we know it. The make-up is a very good one, but we are not to be taken in by it. You must come with us; and so no more talk about it."

"Come along," cried the watchmen, in a chorus; "we ain't going to stay here and chance being scragged by some o' your friends and mates. Come along!"

It was in vain that the chaplain protested; his captors would listen to nothing he had to say.

"The fellow who galloped off with the man across his saddle was a highwayman, and you was with him—that's enough for us."

Mr. Ashton wished to explain the circumstances of the case and relate the history of the unfortunate woman he had tried so hard to save. But he might as well have appealed to savages. All he could get for his pains was the brutal reply that they dared say it was all very fine and clever, but they were down to such trumpery dodges, and were not to be taken in so easily.

Through the streets they hurried their helpless prisoner, and at last brought him to the lock-up in Aldersgate-street.

It was a miserable cage, usually filled with the lowest and most dissolute brawlers.

The morning had now broken, and the inmates of the various cells had fallen into slumber. The stench which arose from their dens was overpowering, and it was with eloquent earnestness that Mr. Ashton begged that he should not be confined in one of them.

"No use, my man," said the principal watchman, "no use at all. We ain't going to give such a desperate bird the chance of flying away. In with yer, and no nonsense, or you'll get but rough usage, I'm thinking."

"Since you will detain me," cried Mr. Ashton, "will you send some one to me whom I can trust to take a packet to Newgate?"

"Oh, Newgate be blowed! shut up your noise and go to sleep."

The door of the cell into which the chaplain was thrust was slammed home, and he was left to his meditations.

Of what description they were the reader can readily imagine.

The life of a human being depended on him, and on him alone.

He had in his possession that which could snatch her from the hangman; and there he was, confined in a noisome dungeon, without the power of stirring hand or foot to snatch her from the inevitable doom which hung over her.

He knew that Jack had secured the real murderer; but that was useless without the production of the reprieve. He blamed himself for the weakness and confusion which led him to disregard Jack's urgent request that he should fly.

"Oh, if I had had the sense of a child," he cried, "I should have evaded these hardened men, and have flown to succour the innocent. Craven heart that I am, to have succumbed thus!"

Alternately upbraiding himself and beating at the door of his cell to attract the attention of those without, the first hour of his imprisonment passed over.

"Alas! alas!" he cried, as the broad daylight burst into his cell, "in another hour or two it will be too late, and she will have suffered. Oh, the child—the poor, innocent, defenceless child!"

The thought was maddening, and it was with renewed energy that the good chaplain applied himself to the task of attracting the attention of those without.

"Men, men!" he cried—"if men you be, pray release me. The sun rises high in the heavens, and ere another hour has passed it will be too late. Release me—release me! Gold, bright gold—all I possess in the world, shall be yours, if you will but open this door and allow me to fulfil my mission."

"Curse your mission!" cried the sleepy and sullen watchmen. Just go to sleep, wil yer, or we'll give yer something that'll make yer."

With this they closed their eyes again, and attempted to resume the slumber from which they had been aroused.

"I implore—I entreat"——

"Shut up, or we'll smash yer head in."

That was the threat which silenced the poor chaplain.

His repeated cries had, however, aroused the inmates of the adjoining cells, and they forthwith commenced a very animated conversation on the very subject which so agitated the chaplain.

It was evident that he was surrounded by a gang of miscreants of the worst order.

"Deuced unlucky to be shut up here, and such a treat going on at Newgate," said one.

"What treat?" asked another.

"What treat? Why the hanging of that woman for the murder of her cousin, to be sure."

"Oh, is that this morning?"

"Yes."

"I shouldn't mind seeing it."

"I'm sure I shouldn't; she deserves it."

"Awful affair, wasn't it?"

"Yes, for a woman to be mixed up in."

"What did she do to the fellow?"

"Oh, a mere trifle."

"What was it? It couldn't have been much of a trifle to kill him."

"Couldn't it? yes it could though; she only dashed out his brains."

"Ha! ha! ha! I wonder if it hurted him."

"Hurted him—o' course not. It must be rather pleasant than otherwise."

"No doubt, but I'd rather him than me."

"So would I. But he's jolly enough now."

"Awfully jolly I should say. I wonder how he likes his companions."

"What companions?"

"Why, the worms, to be sure; they're fellows, only bedfellows in the grave."

"Ho! ho! ho!" roared the other, "that's a good joke."

The blood of the chaplain froze in his veins as he listened to these terrible jests.

They but increased his desire to fly from his bondage, but he was fast held in the noissome den, too fast to move; and still the minutes flitted away, and the terrible hour drew near.

"No hope!" he cried, "no hope!"

"Hillo!" shouted one of the two wretches to whose conversation he had listened, "is there anybody grieving next door?"

"Make no jest of my despair," cried the chaplain; "it is by far too serious a matter for laughter."

"Is it though? Poor old cripple! what are you in for?"

"Do not ask me, for I am too confused to speak."

"Not used to it?"

"No! Heaven in his mercy forbid."

"What a pity! Ah, you see, old sanctimonious, the morning's reflections don't come as pleasant as the night's jollity. I s'pose you got drunk and was caught sleeping in the gutter, or p'raps you were obstreperous and pitched into the watch—eh?"

"No, no; it is nothing of the kind, I assure you."

"Ah, your assurances won't go for much. How much d'ye think he'll get, Bill?"

"First offence?"

"Blest if it don't look like it."

"Then they'll let him off with a month."

"A month's imprisonment!" cried the horrified chaplain. "No, no; it is not so bad as that. But God knows I would willingly undergo that much incarceration, or even more, so that I could save her."

"Hillo! the old fogey is in love."

"Who's the charmer?"

"Cease your badinage," cried the chaplain. "Lawless men, hold no further converse with me, for I am sick at heart, and cannot find words to answer thy brutal remarks."

"Come, I say," shouted one; "no cheek, or when we get out o' this I'll give you one for yourself as you'll remember. Blest if I don't, if I get an extra month for it."

The chairman offered no further reply, and the men left him unmolested.

Another hour passed, and the clock struck the hour of seven.

The deep tone of the bell seemed to clash through the brain of the poor chaplain and madden him.

In imagination he saw the unhappy woman led forth, her child torn from her, and her arms pinioned.

He could hear the shouts of the multitude, and picture the efforts of the executioner as he dragged the poor soul to the scaffold; and there he sat, powerless, helpless, with the reprieve in his pocket! He could have dashed himself to pieces against the rough walls of his cell.

The sound of the clock had barely died away when the clatter of a horse's hoofs fell distinctly on the ears of the minister.

"Heaven bless us;" he cried. "If it should be the highwayman!"

It was the highwayman. Long and tedious had been the search Jack had made for the chaplain, but falling across one of the several watchmen who had assisted in his capture, he was informed of his whereabouts.

The mare was unfailing; in spite of all the fatigue she had undergone throughout that long night she still answered the call of her master, and gallantly obeyed his touch.

In a few minutes after Jack had parted company with the watchman he darted up to the watch-house of Aldersgate-street.

The entrance to the lock-up was a wide one, and Jack hesitated not to ride in, mounted as he was, rather than to leave his mare in the street.

The floor of the little prison was of stone, and of course the mare traversed it easily.

On either side of the passage were the cells; at the extreme end were the rooms appropriated by the guardians of the night.

Jack hesitated not to ride into their very midst.

"Hilloa!" he cried, as the aroused watchmen tumbled off their benches; "hilloa here! You have a prisoner, the chaplain of Newgate; I must see him."

He sprang from the mare as he spoke.

Shaking themselves together, the watchmen rose and stared at the intruder.

It was in all probability the very first time a mounted horseman had dared enter the precincts of their dormitory in the abrupt style adopted by Jack; and the astonishment of the upholders of the law may be imagined.

"Hillo here!" shouted Jack, "are you all deaf? I say, you have a prisoner here, a clergyman."

"And I say we have two prisoners here—a clergyman and a highwayman. Now, what have you to say to that?"

"Nothing in particular, save that I am in no cue for argument or jesting. My business is of too serious a nature."

"Is it, though?"

"It is, man; it is. Will you answer me? Have you not the chaplain of Newgate under lock and key?"

"We have the chaplain of the Minories under lock and key, if that's what you mean."

"Do not mistake. The gentleman of whom you speak is really the chaplain of Newgate, who was in the Minories on a matter of life and death; you must release him instantly."

"Must we? how droll!"

"Fool, I tell you it is in his power to save the woman who is to be hung this morning at Newgate. He has the reprieve and her blood will be upon you if you detain him further."

"Come, none o' that gammon!" said one of the watch; "we can't put up with it, yer know; and if yer think to get away again, you are precious mistaken. We know you."

"Oh, that we do," shouted the others. "Look at his boots—its Sixteen-String Jack! He's a nice one to be looking after the chaplain o' Newgate, he is!"

"I tell you, the words I speak are true. You will not detain me. You will let me see him,—you will let me bear to Newgate the reprieve, if you will not liberate him."

"Look here," said one to the other; "that chaplain cove has some swag about him that they want to get off, and this is the dodge they are down to; but it won't do, Jack; we are too old. Both you and your chaplain will go before the beak before you leave our clutches."

"I tell you I will not be detained."

"And we say, you shall. Come on, men."

They rushed upon Jack with the ferocity of wild beasts, and in a moment had him completely at their mercy.

"Now," said the one who had put so base an interpretation on Jack's motives in coming there, "now let him go in and talk over matters with his friend the parson, and much good may it do them."

Another minute and Jack was thrust into the cell in which the distracted chaplain sat rocking himself to and fro in unutterable anguish.

"You are come!" cried the chaplain—"thank God! you are come!"

"Yes, I am come; but I am useless. I, like yourself, am a prisoner. They would not listen to me, and all is lost."

"Oh, Heaven! Say not so."

"It is so. It is all over now. I have struggled in vain. Jack's word is broken at last."

The poor fellow buried his face in his hands, and gave vent to a flood of tears.

"All over!—all over!" he cried in anguish.

"Nay," said the chaplain, who forgot his own sorrow in that of the highwayman, "do not thus give way to tears. Let us think if something cannot be done."

"Too late! too late!"

"Nay, nay; Heaven will surely interpose for the innocent. Let us not yet despair."

"It is all over. It is ended."

"Since you have come, I feel there is hope yet. I am relieved of half my sorrow."

"Old man," said Jack with awful emphasis "I tell you to give birth to no false hopes. It is ended, I tell you. We are both prisoners. The mare is captured, and in a few minutes the poor woman will be on the scaffold."

"It is horrible!"

"Horrible;" cried Jack, "it is excruciating. Oh, God have mercy upon those fiends if I once get free again, for I will have none!"

"Be not rash."

"Is she not to die? Can I be calm, and she with her foot on the scaffold?"

Crash! Crash! Crash!

The door of the cell fell in, shattered into ten thousand atoms. In the passage Jack beheld his mare dashing out her heels right and left, and laying the band of watchmen to the earth.

The poor brute, with miraculous instinct, had beheld her master made prisoner, and on being led through the passage into the street had taken this mode of assisting him.

"There is hope!" shouted Jack, with a wildness approaching a burst of lunacy. "There is hope! Quick—the reprieve!"

The chaplain handed it to him, and he placed it between his teeth.

"Now," he cried, "I can save her, though a thousand fiends stood in my path!"

Dashing to the earth two men who attempted to stop him, he shouted to the mare to go on.

She obeyed, and actually fought her way to the door, covering the retreat of her master at the same time. In the street Jack sprang upon her back, and with a wild "hurrah!" dashed away.

At his heels, springing their rattles and yelling like madmen, came the whole troop of watchmen.

CHAPTER VI.

THE FATAL MOMENT.

THE clock had tolled the half-hour after seven.

The deputy-governor, accompanied by the gaolers, entered the condemned hole.

Mrs. Malvers was sleeping.

"Poor soul," said the dirty little deputy, as he wiped a tear from his eye, "poor soul! it's all over now. And to think that she was so near being saved!"

"Ah! it is sad. I s'pose there's no hope?"

"Hope! and she has but thirty minutes to live!"

Mrs. Malvers awoke with a scream.

Her cry alarmed her poor little infant, and it commenced a dismal wailing, which was only checked when the mother clasped it to her bosom, and by gentle words reassured it.

She then turned to the group of men who had entered her cell.

"Has he come?" she cried. "Is all well at last?"

The deputy hung his head and answered not.

The poor woman gazed upon him fixedly for a moment, and then her head dropped, and she murmured,—

"You need not speak. I read the answer in your countenance!"

"God bless you, my poor soul," said the old man; "it is my duty to tell you there is no hope."

"No hope!" she repeated, absently, "no hope!"

"It is past the half-hour after seven, and you must leave your cell."

The poor young creature shuddered, and held her babe more closely to her bosom.

"Shall I call in the woman?"

"What woman?"

"The woman who will take your child."

"Take my child?"

"Yes; it is time you parted with it. I should have hastened the separation; but I thought of the possible return of those you expect, and I determined to give you the last chance."

"The last chance!"

"It was the last; all is now over." He turned to the gaoler, and continued, "Call in your wife."

The man did as he was ordered, and a tall and rather ill-favoured woman entered the cell.

The young mother gazed anxiously at her, and turned her eyes away with a shudder.

And it was to such a being her tenderly-cared-for darling was to be handed!

"How shall I part with it?" cried the poor mother; "how can I hand it to another?"

"Painful as the ordeal may be," said the deputy, "it must be done, and speedily. In an adjoining room is the sheriff and the ——" he was about to say hangman, but he hesitated, and said, "officers, who await your coming."

"Yes, yes," she cried, "I know, I know. Give me but a few moments. Oh! you do not know the terrible ordeal a mother undergoes in parting with her only child."

"I do know," said the deputy, "for I have seen it more than once; and therefore I would urge you to be as brief as possible. By delay you will but augment your sorrow."

"You are right," cried Mrs. Malvers, "you are right. Let her—let her take—no, no, no, I cannot spare my babe! Let it be with me till the last. It is but a small request. You will grant it, will you not? and God will bless you."

"I would grant anything you would ask," said the deputy, "if I had but the power to do so; but in this instance I have none. The sheriff would strongly object. Besides, it is usual to pinion the condemned persons before they ascend the scaffold."

"But they will not tear my child from me. A last request—a request so poor and so easily granted—will surely not be refused. They will let my closing eyes rest on my babe. They will do so, will they not? Oh! tell me, tell me they will do so!"

"I dare not tell you that which would be false. They will not allow any such proceeding. Pray calm yourself, and hand the child to the woman. Heaven knows I would spare you, but if you do not hand over your poor babe I must tear it from you."

"Oh, God, that it should come to this!"

She laid her child on her knees, and buried her face in her hands.

The deputy observed the mother's grief, and motioned the woman to bear the child away.

She immediately obeyed, and advancing a step, hastily snatched the babe from its resting-place.

With a loud shriek Mrs. Malvers rose to her feet.

"One look!" she cried, "one last look—but one kiss, and then I will give it you freely. Indeed, indeed, I will!"

"It were best not to prolong the scene," said the deputy; "bear the babe away."

The woman hastened from the cell, and mother and child were separated.

It was a terrible sight, was that of the poor young mother wailing for the loss of the child so dear to her.

Horrible were the feelings which agitated her as she heard the child's cry dying away in the distance, as it was rudely hushed in the arms of the stranger.

The pang of death was nothing compared with the agony of that moment!

It was gone, and the last tie was broken.

After this she consented to be led forth from the cell without further hesitation. In the room where the pinioning was gone through she was met by the sheriff, the officers of the gaol, the second chaplain (in the absence of Mr. Ashton), and *the hangman*.

They all treated her with the utmost consideration, and strove to soothe the great sorrow that was upon her. Even the hangman, hardened by years of practice of his dreadful trade, softened at the sight of the condemned woman.

"It was many years ago," he said, "that I hanged one so young and handsome. It is a bad business, and I'd willingly get out of it, if I could. I don't like hanging women, especially those so like angels."

He spoke of angels! What did the thoughts of that man run on when they were not occupied in matters nearly connected with his daily life? Everything pointed to his thinking of death in its worst forms. It was natural to suppose that one whose trade was that of hangman should have thought of death, and death, too, in its worst phases. Old, bold, strong men struggling with it, with the fatal rope tightened round the muscular throat; of protruding tongues, of eyes starting from their sockets, of swollen faces, and thin blue lines about the throat, of icy hands, of blood, and of the dark grave within the prison walls! This, we say, it would be natural to suppose was the subject which would occupy the leisure moments of such a man; but here was one who, by his spoken words, gave the lie to such a supposition.

"I don't like hanging women, especially those who look so like angels!"

And he, perhaps, dreamt of angels! Fair faces, spotless forms, halos of glory about hair of gold, wings of silver, and robes of spotless white. He must have thought this, or he could not have spoken the words we have noted. And thank God for it! It is well that those whose offices lead them into the darker paths should have some bright spots to look out upon, or humanity would die away, and the brute nature reign paramount in the image of the Maker of mankind.

Well for that man, well for us all, if we could ever think of angels!

Mrs. Malvers gazed about her vaguely. Her head felt light and giddy, and a sickening at the heart and faintness came over her.

" Do your duty," said the sheriff to the executioner.

The man advanced, and went through the operation of pinioning the prisoner.

" You will say you forgive me before you die?" he whispered. " I do not like people to die under my hand and not forgive me. I think of it sometimes, and it does not tend to make me happy."

" I forgive you," said Mrs. Malvers.

" Thank you—thank you!"

The chaplain commenced reading the prayers for the dead, and as the bell tolled the procession was formed, and a movement made for the scaffold.

The first note of the solemn messenger of death, the prison bell, hushed the vast crowd of spectators into silence.

As far as the eye could reach, in the open space before the prison, swarmed a dense mass of humanity, heaving and struggling to get a glimpse of the gallows.

The scene was an awful one. Men, women, and children were there. Beings of the lowest order of humanity—men who thought no more of death than of any of the incidents in the daily routine of the world—women soddened with gin, and deprived of all the more refined feelings of womanhood—and children reared in the lap of filth, educated in the school of crime, graduating for the gallows on which they looked.

The crowd was not wanting in other peculiarities. There were those present who, by their dress and manners, proved themselves to be above the common herd, and whose appearance at that place was perhaps more disgusting than that of the rabble, despite their retiring and unobtrusive behaviour.

It is not a little strange that such an exhibition should have the effect of assembling such an audience. The grave—the mysterious and terrible bourne from which no traveller returns—attracts multitudes to the foot of the scaffold to see a single individual start on the journey; and the subject is made food for wit, ribald jests, and irony. It is the means of affording thousands an excuse for a night's wild debauchery; it hardens the heart; it is a vehicle for the propagation of sin; and yet the institution is permitted to exist now as it did at the time of our story, when England was not the England of to-day, and the untutored minds of our ancestors could tolerate—nay, enjoy—bull and bear-baiting, cock-fighting, and pugilistic encounters between women.

If we cannot do without the hangman, why should he not ply his craft within the prison-walls, away from the gaze of such a crowd as that on which we are now supposed to be looking?

Why should death be made the vehicle for that mad enthusiast to yell forth his denunciations and frantic profanations of the sacred book he holds in his hand? Why should it be the means of drawing together that crowd of wild drunkards who have throughout the night glued their lips to the bottles they have brought with them, and fired their poor weak brains with the contents?

Why should it afford that crew of wild, weird women the chance of shrieking and screaming there, and rendering night hideous by their yells? and why, above all, should it admit of the assemblage of those children, who look on the scene as an excellent jest, and enjoy its horrors as if they were items in a banquet of childish sport?

Who shall answer these questions?

Turn we now to our history.

From midnight the crowd had grown and grown, until its size became alarming, and groans of suffocation and screams of pain went up on all sides.

The streets in the immediate neighbourhood were also full,

and as the hours passed the excitement became fearful to behold.

The crime of which Mrs. Malvers was supposed to be guilty had obtained a vast reputation, and people came from far and near to witness the execution of its projector.

Men wandered about the outskirts of the throng, vending what they termed the " life and confession of the culprit, with the true history of the crime "—a production which had served the turn of the vendors at least a dozen previous executions. These were eagerly bought, and their contents devoured with avidity.

It was a foretaste to whet the appetite for the banquet of horrors which was to follow.

These vendors drove a thriving trade, as did also the proprietors of the public-houses in the neighbourhood, which were crowded on an early hour the previous night.

Rooms commanding a view of the gallows were let at truly fabulous sums, and there the more respectable of the tribe of sensation seekers whiled away the night, relating their experiences of former executions witnessed by them.

Here is a group to whom we may listen.

The speaker is an old man, who " does " the executions for the newspapers.

" I remember the day Tony Harrison was hung; he who killed the four children at Richmond, and then attempted the life of his uncle; don't you remember?"

" I've heard of him."

" Ah! his was something like an execution."

" Was it?"

" That it was. I shall never forget the scene."

" There was something extraordinary happened, wasn't there?"

" I should rather think there was. My! that was a sight to come to see."

" What was it?"

" Why, the rope broke."

" Did it, though?"

" It did; and down came poor Tony with a crash. You should have heard the yell of the crowd."

" Awful, I s'pose?"

" Frightful!"

" Well, was he killed?"

" Not that time. He was horribly mutilated, and his neck was somewhat hurt, but he was far from dead."

" And they hung him up again?"

" Yes, I should say they did; and we had to wait until a fresh rope could be found, which was no small bother, I can tell you."

" It must have been a thing to remember."

" It was. They had to carry him to the scaffold, and hold him under the drop while the hangman went through his performance for the second time."

" That was a sight!"

" It was; but I thought the mob would give way to the feelings which agitated it. Never was there such screaming and riot. They had to keep the hangman within the prison for many weeks. If he had been caught they would have torn him to pieces."

More of these fearful anecdotes followed, and were listened to with the greatest possible interest; and the old man became the hero of his circle.

At length the bell tolled eight, and the stillness we have before alluded to came over the crowd.

A few moments, and the procession mounted the scaffold.

" Hats off!" was the angry roar of those behind who could not get a glimpse of the proceedings.

The surging of the human sea was stilled, and every eye was turned to the fatal spot.

Mrs. Malvers was led to the scaffold, and had to be supported as she stood there.

She was perfectly sensible of her position, but physically she was entirely prostrated.

Her appearance elicited a general murmur of sympathy.

" How young, how beautiful! She doesn't look like one who could commit such a murder."

The poor soul gave one glance at the sea of faces turned upon her.

The sight astounded her, and she turned her gaze heavenward.

The chaplain continued the dull mumbling of the prayers, and the preliminaries were hastily gone through.

" Have you anything to say ? " asked the sheriff, advancing to the side of the poor woman.

" Nothing," she replied, " nothing, save that I am innocent, and that time—perhaps a few short hours—will reveal the whole truth of my oft-repeated assertion."

" It is bad," continued the sheriff, " to quit the world with a falsehood on the lips. If you are guilty, pray confess; remember, you have but a few moments to live."

" I am innocent."

The sheriff withdrew, and the hangman now advanced and drew the white cap over the poor woman's face.

There was a shudder amongst the crowd so visible that the poor woman could hear and feel it.

She prayed that God would deprive her of the sense of hearing and feeling.

The sensations she was experiencing were too much for her, and yet she was painfully alive to all that was taking place. She heard the words of the chaplain, she felt the terrible touch of the hangman, and at last she was moved under the fatal beam.

The rope encircled her throat, and all was prepared.

A hand clasped hers : it was that of the hangman.

" Good-by ! " he said, " you are going to be an angel."

He hurried from the scaffold to draw the fatal bolt.

All was prepared !

Horrible moment of suspense ! Agony ten thousand times concentrated.

The hangman's hand is on the bolt !

*   *   *   *   *   *

" Hurrah ! hurrah ! " The shouting was in the distance.

" Stay your hand," cried the sheriff; " what means that cry ? "

" Hurrah ! hurrah ! Sixteen-String Jack for ever ! Harrah ! hurrah ! "

Nearer and nearer came the shouts.

" What is it ? " cried the sheriff.

" It is Jack," cried the deputy governor, in a fever of excitement. " Call up the hangman; Jack has *a reprieve !* "

The hangman returned once more to the scaffold.

" Look to the woman ; she faints."

" Hurrah ! A reprieve—a reprieve ! "

" Clear a way, clear a way for the bold Jack ! A reprieve —a reprieve ! "

The shout was taken up by ten thousand throats.

Stentorian lungs yelled out the words until the whole air was rent with them.

" Hurrah ! way for Jack ! A reprieve—a reprieve ! "

On the outskirts of the crowd a horseman could be seen ploughing his way into the very midst of the throng.

It was indeed Jack, and in his hand he held above his head the sealed packet from the Secretary of State.

The gallant mare, imbued with the excitement of those about her, snorted proudly, and ploughed on through the crowd as if conscious of her own importance and that of her bold rider.

" Bold Jack, brave Jack ! " cried the excited mob. " Jack's the man ; room, room ; fall back ; let him reach the prison ! "

" Hurrah for Jack ! He has saved the woman."

" Make way there," cried the horseman, glancing up at the scaffold, " make way ; it is death to delay me a second ; I bear a reprieve ! "

There was not much occasion for him to shout.

The crowd, a few moments ago thirsting for the scene of death, were now mad with frantic delight at the thought of the miraculous escape of the intended victim.

The men fell back as well as they were able, and made a lane for the horseman straight to the prison.

He was there in a few moments, and the ponderous gates opened for him.

He was within, and everyone hurried from the scaffold.

Mrs. Malvers was carried away dead faint.

The excitement had been too much for her, and she had succumbed.

In a few moments the sheriff had read the reprieve, and satisfying himself as to his validity, ordered that every care should be taken of the prisoner until the search of the house of Malvers had been completed.

" If it is as the accomplice reports the woman must at once be set at liberty. There can be no excuse for detaining her."

" Free ! " said Jack, " free ! and by my own contriving. Thank God, I have kept my oath."

" You are a brave fellow, Jack," said the deputy-governor, " a very brave fellow ; and it is with regret that I am obliged to address you as my prisoner."

" Never mind," said Jack, " I have not broken my word, and that is everything. I suppose it will be my turn to mount your scaffold next. Well, it's a bad end, but it can't be helped now. Tell them, though, that I gave myself up to justice, and don't let them think worse of me than you can help ; and above all, be kind to my poor mare. She will not trouble anyone for long when I'm gone, poor old girl ! When she misses my hand she will pine away and die."

" Come, Jack, cheer up ! You're not dead yet."

CHAPTER VII.

SHOWS WHY MR. PETER PATTYPAN MADE SOME CONFECTIONS.

ANY ONE in the habit of passing through Holborn at the date of this story, would not have failed to notice a very neat confectioner's shop not far from the brow of the hill.

The place was very clean, and the window dressed with all manner of tempting morsels, set out with an eye to effect.

True, at that time shop-windows did not admit of the display we note in the present epoch of history. Gigantic sheets of plate-glass were not as yet dreamt of, and interiors dazzling with marble, mirrors, and gold mouldings were only to be found in the mansions of the great, and there only rarely.

Nevertheless, the shop of Mr. Peter Pattypan was an extremely natty place, and, the small squares of glass and limited space excepted, really presented a very striking appearance.

Fine jellies and preserves were well exhibited ; sweets were ranged in long bottles, with due regard for the laws of harmony of colours, and ices were represented by very tolerable imitations ranged in rows of glasses, and looked remarkably tempting in the summer, but in the winter were suggestive of anything but pleasurable sensations in the stomach.

In the window of Pattypan's shop was exhibited a large placard, on which was depicted in gold letters the following announcement :—

PETER PATTYPAN,
PASTRYCOOK AND CONFECTIONER.
Wedding Breakfasts provided. Balls, Routs, Pic-nics, &c., attended.

This card was the constant delight of Peter.

He used to view it from all points of observation. He would change its position half-a-dozen times a day in his endeavours to improve its effects on the passers-by ; it was, in fact, Peter's hobby, and to him a never-failing source of gratification and amusement. Never was there such an enthusiastic pastrycook as Peter ; he was really wedded to his business, and he certainly proved a very attentive and enthusiastic spouse.

His thoughts were confined to his shop, and his whole life was a long, uninterrupted dream of pastry and confections.

Peter was a little man of rather singular appearance. He bore about him the look of a confectioner. There was something in his face suggestive of cake and jelly. Jams appeared to be marked on his lips, and certainly nothing but sugar was in his voice, for a more even tempered, better disposed little man than Peter could not be found in a day's ramble. He was

JACK AND THE DEPUTY-GOVERNOR.

always nattily dressed in a light suit of clothes, over which he wore a white apron, sleeves, and cap, so bright and snowy that they gave one the idea of being kept in flour, washed in milk and glossed over with the whites of eggs rather than the iron of the laundress.

Such, then, was Peter's shop, and such was Peter.

It is only necessary to add that Peter was a bachelor, and that the best part of his well-furnished little house was let out as lodgings. His establishment was ruled over by a mild old lady, as harmless and pleasant as Peter himself, and who was assisted by a tall, raw-boned girl of about fifteen years, who was taken out of the workhouse by Peter, and whom he there-fore named Charity; her surname was Dobbs. The peculiarity of this specimen of humanity was, as she expressed it, "that she was a orphin, and that she hadn't got no mem'ry; but she couldn't help that—cos why, warn't she brought up in a work'us?"

Charity Dobbs was allowed to have pretty much her own way in the establishment of Pattypan, but she had an awful enemy in Sam Snike's, Pattypan's apprentice and errand-boy, a juvenile with an overpowering propensity for leaping over street-posts, and keeping mice, rabbits, and guinea-pigs. He was, moreover, addicted to substituting the "v" for "w," and talking the most abominable Cockney English ever heard.

Sam was a legitimate street-boy of the period, and was never so happy as when sent on a long errand, so that he might enjoy himself by performing on the posts, worrying inoffensive dogs and cats, and playing at the games usually indulged in by boys of his class in the by-ways of large towns.

Sam, as we have said, was the sworn enemy of Charity Dobbs. He taunted her with her failings, accused her of having faults she never possessed, frightened her into fits with his small menagerie, and when not otherwise engaged, chevied her from the top of the house to the bottom, with an enthusiastic enjoyment of the sport worthy the keenest huntsman in the pursuit of his favourite pastime.

Now that we have done with Peter's house and household let us turn to his lodgers.

At the period of which we write Peter's best rooms were engaged by a lady and her infant son; in a word, it was Mrs Malvers and her child.

Released from Newgate, she was brought to Peter by the excellent chaplain, and the kind-hearted little pastrycook received her and treated her as gently as if she had been his own child.

Peter exerted himself strenuously to add to the comforts and happiness of his guest, and her smiles repaid him for his care.

"And ample payment, too," he used to say; "it does one's heart good to get her to smile. Poor thing! she hasn't much cause for mirth."

The baby, too, was a source of great joy to him. He was never tired of extolling its merits to those with whom he came in contact. Sam he put down as a barbarian, because he created so much noise in his recreation of worrying Charity up and down stairs.

"Poor little boy!" Peter used to say, "I wonder he can ever get a wink of sleep with that scoundrel flying about the

www.ingramcontent.com/pod-product-compliance
Lightning Source LLC
Chambersburg PA
CBHW082054220626
47052CB00006B/1240